BOSTON JONSON IN
MURDER BY ART

Biff Mitchell

BOSTON JONSON IN
MURDER BY ART

DOUBLE DRAGON

Chapter 1

"True art is immune to the viewer," she said. Her name was WhiteFeather. Just WhiteFeather. She was an artist, a fiber artist to be precise, who used an unusual combination of fibers in her art - bones, animal skulls, human hair, menstrual blood, souls of found objects, unusual stuff. The three hundred pound corpse nailed to the wall was also an artist. He painted beer cans, but that wasn't his real art. WhiteFeather looked disgustedly at the big man hanging on the wall. "He'd get drunk and go on and on about his life itself being a work of art in progress." She shook her head. "Well, thank God he finally finished it."

She walked back to her studio, ducking under a snakeskin chandelier, real snakeskin. Boston couldn't help noticing that she had a nice ass. After all, it was his job to notice things. She also had a wide mouth lit up with the brightest red lipstick he'd ever seen, but it suited her dark hair and eyes. He was tempted to tell her that she was a fine work of art, but he was here on business. He had a referral to make, and it looked like he was going to be up to his neck in shit again, but that was his choice. This was just the kind of referral he loved - weird, like him. Like, how often did you get a referral for a three hundred pound work of human art hanging on the wall of the most notorious art studio in the city, infamous for wild parties and wilder artists. Juicy.

"More like somebody finished it for him," said Boston. The dead guy's name was Art Cranbury. He owned the century and half old building that housed

Studio4Ward, a former dance hall, now broken into four open studios shared by three hot stuff comers in the art world and one cold stiff that was soon to be hot stuff in the webloids. Apparently, the stiff had been a pain in the ass. "How long has he owned the building?"

WhiteFeather looked up from a leather moccasin from which she was extracting metal staples with a pair of pliers. "For the last six months. We thought it would be cool at first, having the building owner in here as one of us." She tugged a particularly stubborn staple. It came out with a small tearing sound. "As one of us, maybe he'd lower the rent, put in air conditioning." She pointed up to the ceiling at a circular opening about eight feet in diameter with ornate wooden struts radiating from the center. There was one in each corner of the studio. "Those fans just push the hot air around. On a hot day, this place is a furnace." She pulled out another stubborn piece of metal with a loud chunk sound. "Who the hell makes moccasins with staples?" she asked herself angrily.

"But having him here didn't work out?"

"The opposite." She rested the pliers and moccasin in her lap and looked up at Boston. "He lied about being an artist. That's his studio over there." She pointed to a corner with a heavy duty beach chair surrounded by beer cans, empty pizza boxes, and stains that looked like dried barf. An easel holding a child-like painting of a beer can faced out from his studio. All of Studio4Ward was cluttered, but Cranbury's corner was filthy. "He was here almost every night, getting drunk, belching, farting, leering. The other two artists are women. We made a point of never being alone when he was here, and he was here most of the time. He passed out in his chair a lot, and stayed the night. He did that for over a week once. Went downstairs once or twice a day for beer and pizza deliveries. We had to plant air fresheners all over the place because the smell of him was sickening."

"Karma," said Boston.

"Beg your pardon?" She looked puzzled. After thinking a moment, she looked at Boson irritably. "Even if we'd told him he couldn't move in... he owned the building. He could have moved in without our permission, or raised the rent, or just make life miserable for us in other ways." She went back to pulling staples, but now with strong, angry tugs.

Boston turned back to the man on the wall. Art Cranbury was massive. He was nailed up Christ-like, hands open and nailed pretty much where Boston assumed the nails in Christ's hands would have been. His head was propped by another nail, more accurately, a spike. Same for his feet - crossed at the ankles and spiked together. The only difference between Cranbury and Christ - besides size and sainthood - was that Art Cranbury had been nailed up backwards. And he was naked. Two enormous mounds of ass fat drooped from the center of his body, which had been painted with red and white stripes, barber pole style.

It was time to get into the vibes of this place. Boston had a theory about vibrations. They were at the core of all being, the building blocks of

7

Creation. Come into contact with the vibrations of a place and your imprint would be left on them like aftershave in a breezeless hall, which meant that Art Cranbury's last minutes on Earth lurked in the vibrations in this room. Boston closed his eyes and slowed his breathing, taking the air deep into his tan dien - the area behind his belly button that served as a powerhouse of spiritual and psychic energy - expelling it slowly, evenly. He dropped his shoulders and let his awareness sink into his belly button. He cleared his mind of clutter and entered the void. A deep low hum originating in his throat moved up into his sinus cavity, emanated from his nostrils. He stood by the body, ignoring its stench, and searched the stuff of Creation for clues.

As usual, nothing happened.

WhiteFeather watched him, still tugging staples. Her expression said it all: she'd rather be extracting wisdom teeth from his jaws.

He had that effect on people. After all, he was Boston Jonson, Creme de la Crop of the CI fold - a Consultative Investigator, society's filter between crime and the cops. His job was to be first in, check it out, and make a referral for anything from a full scale murder investigation to no further action required, or somewhere in between, like bring in the social workers and shamans or let the media handle this one. They sent him to snoop and refer - something he rarely did, being notorious for outstaying his welcome and acting the proverbial shit stirrer. But the webloids loved him - with eye-catching shoulder length tangerine hair, aqua eyes, square movie star jaw and a penchant for colorful

Hawaiian hula-hula shirts, he looked just offbeat enough to capture the public's imagination.

He stood on his toes and craned his neck around the dead man's head. Having never met anyone weirder than himself, Boston was seldom shaken by anything he saw on the job, but what he saw now raised his eyebrows. The dead man's eyes were wide open, but not with horror. The zany smile on his face suggested joy, happiness, bliss - like he'd died getting his jollies off. This was getting weirder by the minute. He loved it.

Boston's wallet buzzed. It was Laurel from Central CI. He snapped his wallet open and saw the familiar woman's head on the tiny screen. "Boston," she said. "They want quick and dirtless on this one. The skinny is, Arthur Cranbury was an asshole, but a very rich asshole. Old money. Old family. He was the black sheep. The family would like his memory to just pass away with him. These people are powerful, Boston."

"They're always powerful," said Boston into his wallet.

The face in the wallet looked annoyed. "Who's always powerful, Boston?"

"Old moneyed families."

"That has nothing to do with anything except you need to just make your referral and get the hell out of there. Even the police are going to cooperate on this one - maybe call it suicide."

"Laurel," said Boston, staring at the body on the wall. "He was nailed face-first to a wall with spikes and nails in his hands, head, and ankles. Then he was painted like a candy cane."

9

"Some people like to get creative with their suicides. Make your referral."

"Just a couple of things I have to check out."

"Boston!"

"I'll get back to you." He snapped his wallet shut, cutting off a loud "Bost... !" and stuffed it into his shirt pocket. It buzzed immediately, but he ignored it. He noticed several dolls on the wall behind WhiteFeather. The heads appeared to be skulls of small animals and the hair flowing down from their heads looked human. "Into the death thing?" he asked, pointing at the dolls.

WhiteFeather glared at him. "Into the life thing. The dolls are reminders of the cycle of life. It includes death. Shouldn't you just be following orders like the woman in your wallet said, and make your referral so that we can all just go back to normal?"

He ignored her question. "Did he have enemies?"

She cocked her head in the question mark pose, eyes and mouth wide, but instead of saying 'duh' she said, "Haven't you heard anything anybody's told you? The woman on the phone said his entire family wants him forgotten. She called him an asshole. I told you what he's been doing to the artists here. Everybody in the building wants him gone!"

Boston raised an eyebrow. "Everybody in the building?"

She pushed out a loud sigh. "See that stereo system behind his chair?" Boston looked where she was pointing and saw an old pre-2020 nano-enhanced mini-system. The get-up would fit into your cupped hands, but it blasted out a thousand watts of ear splitting sound. "He cranked it so loud that everybody in the building could hear, and all he ever played was Lou Reed's Metal Machine Music. He played it over and over and over. Eric threatened to kill him once." She stopped short. "But he didn't really mean it. It was just rhetorical."

"What did he say?"

"Keep it up and I'll kill you."

"Hmm," mused Boston. "Rhetorical."

"Eric can be gruff at times," said WhiteFeather, picking up the pliers and moccasin again. "But he's not a murderer. He would never kill anybody."

"And just who is Eric?" said Boston nonchalantly, but feeling like a bloodhound catching a whiff of prey. *Could it be this easy?*

"Just because you say you're going to kill somebody, doesn't mean that you mean it," she said, snapping a staple angrily.

"Then he'll be OK. Who is he?"

"Eric Hill. He owns a music store downstairs." She pointed the pliers in a direction through the floor and off to Boston's left. "Backstreet records. He sells plastic records to audiophiles." She let go of the moccasin and pliers, clasped her hands and let them settle in her lap. "He's had to come up here over and over to tell Art to turn the music down. I mean, Lou Reed's Metal Machine Music. Eric's customers are serious audiophiles. They come in and hear that garbage blasting down the stairs, and they turn around and leave. Eric said that Art was driving his customers away, putting him out of business."

"So why didn't he just leave? Set up business somewhere else?"

"This building is special," said WhiteFeather. "We all love this place. There isn't anything like it anywhere else in the city. To get in here, we all had to sign five-year leases, and we have two more years to go. If we move out before then, we lose our deposits."

"How much are the deposits?"

"Five thousand dollars."

Boston whistled. "Big deposits."

"They let us pay on them over the first two years."

"Is Hill in now?"

"He's always in," said WhiteFeather, picking up her work again. "He practically lives in his shop. It's down the stairs, to your right. Oh, and from now on... " She closed the pliers on a staple tightly and twisted it out of the moccasin almost violently. "... keep your eyes off my ass."

Chapter 2

Backstreet Records was a strange little shop, modeled as far as Boston could figure after head shops and hippie stores in the last century, long before he'd been born. The walls were plastered with anything that could be nailed, stapled, taped, glued or tacked to a surface - covers from ancient vinyl record albums, posters of vaguely familiar rock stars long since buried by free downloads and desktop studios. There were music CDs with psychedelic imprints, and actual vinyl records. Makeshift wooden shelves and tables holding CDs, books, buttons and pins with pictures of dead musicians were either nailed to the walls or pushed up against them. Wherever the walls weren't covered with something straight, angled or upside down, pre-historic paint peeled and flaked through the memorabilia.

The place smelled like vintage old store.

On the door frame beside Boston's head, swatches of white paper with colored marker ink announced, 'OUT FOR A MOMENT - BACK BY 3:07 PM' 'OUT FOR A MOMENT - BACK BY 2:43 PM.' There were maybe fifty of them tacked and taped together for half the height of the door. For the inexact, there was a single large orange piece of cardboard with big black letters - 'DON'T WORRY, WE'LL BE RIGHT BACK.'

In the center of the shop stood the heart of the business - big wooden bins full of vinyl music albums. Boston walked over to one of them. The albums were stacked against each other like folders

13

in a filing cabinet. He flipped through them. The covers were mostly faded, scratched or torn. He assumed the musicians on the wither surfaces were long gone. None of their names rang bells.

Backstreet records evoked sense of fun and playfulness while at the same time demanding to be taken seriously.

Time to get into the core of this place.

He closed his eyes and relaxed his shoulders. He dropped his awareness into his stomach and let all thoughts about Art Cranbury and Studio4Ward evaporate into a space labeled 'OUT FOR A MOMENT - BACK AT 3:09 PM.' He savored the staleness in the old building's air, the smell of old plastic and aged paper, the reek of rotting beams and deteriorating wires behind the time-eaten walls. He let his being sink into the primal stuff of existence - the vibrations. They were alive and humming, spilling their message into the air around him. He allowed his mind and soul to drift into their hum, and their hum became the music of himself and a low hum carried from the bottom of his abdomen and up through his chest and into his throat where it meant absolutely nothing to Boston, but meant that he was probably a little whacked to the two men standing at the counter a few feet away from him.

One of them, a swarthy man with thick black hair and a full black beard in a black t-shirt was obviously Eric Hill, the shop's owner - he was on the other side of the counter. There was a certain indefinable madness in his dark eyes. Perhaps the madness of too much information about dead musicians? The other man was geeky looking, with a mole-like face, wearing a checked, short-sleeved shirt. They stared at him, their faces a mixture of curiosity and irritation. Boston had that effect on people.

"Hello," he said. "I'm Boston Jonson, CI. I'm referring on a dead person nailed to the wall upstairs."

Their expressions didn't change. Maybe they didn't read the webloids, or maybe they were hard cases. Time to stir it up. He looked the dark-haired shop owner straight in the eyes. "Did you threaten to kill Art Cranbury?"

That changed his expression. The curiosity melted away, leaving pure irritation. "No," he said, flatly.

"WhiteFeather says different," said Boston, smiling sardonically.

Hill scowled as he thought. "I might have said it in a roundabout way. Art was a pain in the ass. Sometimes he could get to you."

"Is that why you killed him?"

The geeky customer slithered away from the counter and popped up by the record bins on the far side of the shop. Hill's face transformed into a battleground of warring emotion, with anger gunning down shock while stunned disbelief flanked *What me*? Slowly, his face calmed, leaving one unified emotion: dark brooding. "I didn't kill him. I'll admit, I fantasized it every day, but I didn't kill him."

Boston noticed something behind the brooding man. What was it? Something about the tall,

15

uncurtained window? The lush green boughs of what looked like Dutch Elm scraping against the glass? Something about the wall around the window? The records tacked to the wall? The notes and price lists? The poster?

The poster.

Tacked up beside the window was a black and white poster looking down on the city of Rio De Janeiro. At the summit of a rock outcropping overlooking the harbor was a statue of Christ with his arms outspread and looking down on the city. His back faced the viewer.

Someone had painted red and white stripes on him. Boston kept this revelation to himself. "Do you paint?"

Hill narrowed his eyes questioningly. "Do I what?"

"Never mind. How well did you know the deceased?"

Hill cupped his left hand over his right fist in front of his chest and cocked his head to one side, looking almost melancholy in a contemplative way. "The same as everyone else in this building, I guess - too well. He drank a lot and when he was drunk, he became obnoxious. He'd come down here and harass my customers, tell them to get their sorry asses into the Twenty-first Century. He owned the place. There was nothing I could do about it."

The mole-faced customer perked up and looked like he was going to say something, but decided to thumb through albums instead.

"He played Lou Reed's Metal Machine Music incessantly," said Hill. "Day and night. Loud. Loud enough that everybody on the second and first floors could hear it. Have you ever heard Metal Machine?"

Boston nodded no.

"It's like... nothing. Just noise. No balance or rhythm or anything. Just irritating, meaningless noise. He played it loud enough that it started to drive my customers away. The people who come here are serious audiophiles. Their ears and appreciation of music are finely tuned mechanisms that are easily offended by the kind of trash Art played. It's painful to them, like auditory torture."

Auditory torture. Boston filed that one in the back of his head for future use. "So you threatened to kill him," said Boston matter-of-factly.

Hill narrowed his eyes on Boston, a certain madness brewing indefinably in their corneal depths. "I didn't threaten to kill him."

"What, exactly, did you say to him?"

Hill thought a moment and said, "Keep it up and I'll kill you." He thought for another moment. "It was rhetorical."

"How did you get him onto the wall?"

Hill looked confused. "I don't know what you're talking about."

"He must weigh something like three hundred pounds." Boston eyed Hill from his feet to his head. "You're big, but not that big. How did you get those three hundred pounds of deadweight up on the wall?"

Hill looked like he was about to spring on Boston, and Boston was sure that, if he turned the heat up just one more notch, steam would blow out both the man's ears. "Aren't you just supposed to make a referral," said Hill, "and get the hell out of the way so that the professionals can do their job?"

Familiar words to Boston Jonson. He let them bounce into the shop's stale air and said, "I'll be upstairs for a while. Stick around. I may have more questions."

Hill glared at Boston as he walked out, a glare that might have killed in some other reality.

Chapter 3

The hall outside Backstreet Records was wide, as were the stairs - erected during an age when buildings were constructed for people. The white walls were accented with brownish red trim, giving them an aged, but well cared for look. The hall led to a glass-paned door with a sign on it: Mazerolle Gallery. *Yep*, he thought, *this place is full of art*. There were no blinds or curtains covering the door's big window, and there were no lights on inside. A 'CLOSED' sign hung from the doorknob. Vaguely, Boston could pick out a few large canvasses hanging on the walls. Across the hall, a flight of stairs led up to the top floor and Studio4Ward.

He heard the sound of women's voices coming from the stairway leading down to the first floor entrance. He walked over and leaned against the balustrade, looking down at two very hot women climbing hurriedly up the stairs. When they reached the top, the taller of the two, a beautiful woman with shoulder length dark hair and a light sprinkling of freckles on her nose and cheeks, regarded him with a look of half recognition, and then her dark eyes lit up. "You're Boston Jonson!" Even with her voice just two octaves short of a shriek, it poured through the air like hot soup. "Boston Jonson, the famous CI!"

He took an immediate liking to her and the sultry 'dare-you' look in her eyes. Before he could say anything, she jumped in. "The Kilburn Blind Man murder referral was the most brilliant investigation ever. I mean, thirty naked pagan women. I heard they might be making a movie about it, with you as the lead character!"

Time to perpetuate the legend and be the cool one. "And you are?" he asked, flat voiced and flat faced. She looked at Boston questioningly, obviously taken aback by his cool brusqueness. Then her face loosened and she giggled. "So the webloids *are* true. You *are* a dickhead when you're making a referral."

He couldn't remember reading that in the webloids. "And *you* are?" he repeated brusquely.

"She's Andrea Crabbe," said the other woman. "Is Art really dead?" She said it without emotion, like asking if it was going to rain later on.

Boston gave her the quick once over. She was shorter than the other, but a knockout with long dark hair, big brown eyes and a full-lipped mouth that bordered on pouty and kiss-me-quick. "And you are?"

"She's Marie Fox," said Crabbe. She'd ditched some of the exuberance. Boston had that effect on his fans. "We're both Studio4Ward artists. WhiteFeather just called and said that Art's been murdered."

"We won't know that until I've made my referral," said Boston.

"You mean he's still alive?" asked Fox, a little too incredulous thought Boston.

"I mean he's officially not dead or alive until I make a referral," said Boston with the emotional non-commitment of a Zen master.

"WhiteFeather said that he was nailed to the wall and painted red and white," said Crabbe, deadpan. "He has a spike through his head."

Boston could feel another fan drifting away after meeting the CI behind the headlines. "Maybe the three of us should go up to the studio. I have questions."

Fox frowned. She obviously didn't like him.

He was used to it.

Chapter 4

"Hi, Art!" said Crabbe cheerfully to the dead man on the wall. "What's up?"

Still seated, WhiteFeather put a finger to her lips and chuckled. "What's up!" she repeated. "What's up, Andrea?"

Crabbe roared, "Art's up!"

Both women burst into laughter. Fox actually cracked a small smile. Obviously, Art Cranbury wasn't going to be missed.

"When you ladies are finished laughing at the dead guy, I have some questions," said Boston in his most business-like tone.

The three ladies looked at him as though he had just snapped into the room from some alternate reality and then they broke into laughter again. Fox joined them this time. Boston let them go on for a few minutes before saying, "The sooner I get my referral done, the sooner I'm out of here, and the sooner... " He pointed his thumb at the corpse. "... you're rid of the stiff."

The laughing subsided quickly. Boston looked at Crabbe. "He's hanging in your studio, Ms Crabbe."

She looked at him with a mixture of amusement and suspicion. "You think I murdered him?" She let out a quick *what the*? breath. "We all hated Art." Subdued laughter from WhiteFeather. "But none of us are killers. And... " She gave the body a disgusted look. "... red and white candy stripes? I mean, we're artists here. We create art. That's... just... Art." She broke into laughter along with

WhiteFeather. Fox put a hand over her mouth, covering an uncontrollable smile. Boston fought back an urge to laugh himself. He let the ladies get it all out, rationalizing that it might be some form of post murder-by-art stress thing. When the laughter finally settled, he looked Crabbe straight in the eye. "Why do you think Eric Hill would want to frame you?"

Her face ignited with shock. She started to say something, but stopped and breathed deeply. She let the air out slowly before speaking. "Nobody's framing me. Look around." She waved a finger around the studio. "All the walls are covered, even Art's." She was right. The walls in WhiteFeather's studio were covered with dolls and other hangings. Fox's walls were covered with paintings and drawings. Art's walls displayed the childlike paintings of beer cans, not hung, but nailed at skewed angles, sometimes one on top of another. "Except mine," she said. "I just finished a major piece and took it down after it dried. That's why he was put up here." She pointed at Art. "It's the only space left to hang anything." She stood, facing Boston defiantly and smiling smugly, as if to say, "So what now, dickhead?"

"Convenient," he said.

"What?"

"You just happened to have a spot to hang Art... " He smiled sardonically for the second time in one day. "... after murdering him."

She narrowed her eyes. Her face flushed. She scowled. *Yep*, thought Boston, *another fan gone*. She was just about to say something when he cut

23

her off. "And how did you get him to smile like that? Looks like his last few minutes on Earth were the biggest romp of his life."

"You asshole!" Crabbe was furious now. "What the hell is *that* supposed to mean?" Even angry, her voice was like hot soup pouring through air.

"Take a look at his face." He pointed at the corpse's head.

All three ladies hurried over to the corpse, standing on tip toes and craning to get a view of Cranbury's face.

"Gross!"

"Oh, geez!"

"Eeuk!"

They backed away, like avoiding dog shit on the sidewalk.

WhiteFeather was first to speak. "Nobody in this studio would ever dream of putting a smile like that on Art Cranbury's face." She looked at the other two. "I think I speak for us all when I say, we'd rather slit our wrists." Crabbe and Fox nodded, disgust clouding their faces as they stared at the back of the dead man's head. "We hated him, Jonson. But none of us killed him. And after seeing his face, I think you can be pretty damn sure it wasn't Eric."

"Maybe he liked to be tickled," said Boston.

WhiteFeather rolled her eyes and went back to her studio. Fox marched past Boston, harrumphing sharply under his nose. *Perky little thing. Maybe I'll torment her next.*

Crabbe glared at Boston over the tops of her comely freckles. "Art had lots of enemies," she said.

24

"If you want some really good suspects, you might want to look at his family. He was an embarrassment to them." She thought for a moment and said, excitedly. "And they have the money to get rid of him. They could have hired somebody to do this... "

"The murderer is in this building," said Boston flatly.

"And just how do you know that?" WhiteFeather was back to pulling staples.

Boston smiled sardonically for the third time in one day. "Just a feeling, mam, just a feeling."

WhiteFeather shot out a loud, disgusted sigh. "You're not even supposed to be here. You're just supposed to come in, look around, make a referral, and get the hell out."

Coincidentally, Boston's wallet started buzzing. It was Laurel. She was pissed. "Make your damn referral, Boston, and get the hell out of there."

"Not quite ready yet, Laurel. Just one loose end to tie up."

"Boston!" Laurel's voice shook Boston's wallet with rage. "Walk over to the window."

"Which one? There's two."

"Either one. Do it now!"

Boston ducked under the snakeskin chandelier and strolled over to a tall narrow window with a ledge large enough to be a small tabletop. He looked outside. "What am I looking for?"

"See that red brick building on the other side of the street?"

"Yep."

"That's the police station. There's three cops in there waiting to cross the street and tie up this whole Art Cranbury thing and just make it go away. They're waiting for your referral. And they're getting very pissed."

"Bullshit. I know the cops in this area. They're drinking coffee and eating donuts, and hoping I take forever."

"Their coffee machine's broken."

"Damn."

"Get that referral in, Boston. Get it... "

He closed his wallet and turned to WhiteFeather. She smiled maliciously at him. "Going to be out of here soon?"

"When my job's done." He walked back to Crabbe's studio. She stood, arms on hips, glaring at him. *How soon they change*. "You know, if you just make your referral, I can get this dead body off my wall and get some work done."

Boston ignored her. What the hell, she wasn't a fan anymore. "Ms Fox!" he called, staring at the corpse. The young artist looked up from a canvas over which she was spreading a layer of light red oil paint. "What?" she said irritably.

"How did you get his body up there?"

"What?" yelled all three ladies in unison.

Chapter 5

After a barrage of verbal abuse so furious that Boston wasn't sure who said what or what exactly was said, the voices lulled gradually into a fuming silence. For the fourth time in one day, Boston smiled sardonically, or maybe it was more like a smirk. "Just throwing it out there. Nothing personal."

WhiteFeather stood up quickly, eyes glowering. "Nothing personal! You just accused her of murder! You don't just throw shit like that out there!"

He felt something on his right hip and suddenly he was almost tumbling, barely managing to right himself. Crabbe had just hipped him, powerfully. Somberly, she shuffled toward a table littered with tubes of acrylic paint, paint encrusted brushes, and other implements of painting. She was calmer than WhiteFeather, but she didn't look like she was going to be a Boston Jonson fan again anytime soon. "Instead of accusing a one hundred and five pound artist of murdering and nailing up a three hundred pound waste of space, you could just make your stupid referral so that I can get that bag of shit off my wall and get back to work."

"Sorry to be an inconvenience, Ms Crabbe, but like I said, the murderer is in this building." He rubbed his hand on the part of his hip where Crabbe had hit him with her hip. It was sore. "And by the way, hipping a CI is a serious offense, punishable by up to five hours of community service."

The young artist peered at Boston with something like amusement dancing in her eyes. "I didn't realize the penalty was so harsh. Please don't report me, Mr Celebrity CI."

"Just be glad that she didn't put you through the wall," said WhiteFeather. "Andrea has the meanest hips in town." Crabbe smiled at Boston and tweaked an eyebrow. "She put a guitar player in the hospital last Halloween with just one mighty movement of those hips. And she's right. We all have work to do here, and having that... " She thumbed at the stiff on the wall. "... thing up there is a distraction."

Boston looked in Fox's direction. She'd been strangely silent for someone who'd just been accused of murder. She stood in front of her canvas, red tipped brush in hand, glaring at Boston. *Too mad to speak*. He let it go.

"I think I'll go downstairs and torment your audiophile friend some more," he said. "I'd appreciate you three hanging around for a while."

"We'd appreciate you getting that stinking mess of asshole out of our studio," said WhiteFeather.

Boston turned to her. The look on his face could almost be described as one of great personal offense. "I'm surprised that an artist of your stature could be so insensitive, Ms WhiteFeather. Art Cranbury was, after all, a human being."

It would be an understatement to use the word incredulity to describe the looks that spread over the faces of the three artists of Studio4Ward. It would also be an understatement to say that Boston Jonson could, on occasion, be so full of shit that his aqua eyes might turn brown.

Chapter 6

The audio geek was gone, replaced by three swarthy old ladies wearing black t-shirts with florescent Gothic lettering spelling out Metallica, Grand Funk Railroad and Kiss. Their arms were tattooed and their hair dyed pink, blue and green. They looked like every biker's momma.

They ignored Boston with the quietly fuming confidence of three elderly women just waiting to trounce the unwary. He walked to the counter where Hill sat on a stool, eyeing him suspiciously, broodingly. He stood as Boston neared the counter. There was questioning in his eyes, an air of *what now*?

Boston leveled his gaze at Hill. *Are those the beginnings of sweat beads on his forehead? Does this man have something to hide?* He pointed at the poster behind Hill. "Who painted Christ?"

Hill cocked his head to one side, bewildered. "What?"

"The poster." Boston wagged his pointing finger. "Somebody painted candy stripes on the Christ statue. Who?"

Hill turned to the poster, stooping slightly to gaze at the statue overlooking the harbor. "This poster used to be on the wall by the door," he said. "Anybody could have done this."

"What's that just below the statue? The red smudge."

Hill stooped further. "Looks like the letter 'M' done with the same marker as the one on the statue."

Boston's eyes flashed. "M? As in murder?"

Hill rolled his eyes, exasperated. "Maybe M as in somebody's initial. Why is this so damned important?"

Boston gazed at Hill with the condescension of someone in touch with the vibrations of reality. "Mr. Hill, you're not qualified to be asking questions during a referral. That would be me." He let that sink in, waiting for Hill's angry glare to shrivel to an irritated glare. "You say it was on the wall by the door?"

"That's right." Yes, there it was, that tone of irritation that Boston so loved to inspire.

"Anyone could have done the drawing?"

"Anyone."

"And what would that letter look like upside down?"

Hill looked confused, glanced at the poster again, and said, "Maybe a W. I don't know. What's this all... ?"

Boston put both hands on the counter and leaned forward. With his flashing aqua eyes and bright orange hair flowing over his hula hula shirted shoulders, Boston Jonson could look formidable leaning forward. Hill backed up a step, surprise in his face. Boston fixed his eyes on him, hard, cold, determined. "Do you have any idea why WhiteFeather would try to frame you for the murder of Art Cranbury?"

***

Standing in the hall, smelling the musky scent of old wood and sensing the passage of thousands of people through the offices and stores that had occupied the building spanning a period of over a century and a half, Boston felt ready to tap into the historical record etched into the frequencies of the vibrations that hummed in this place. He closed his eyes, imagining young women in evening dresses, excited and laughing, on their way up to the dance hall, followed by young men in suits and ties and cream slicked hair. He saw serious men with horn-rimmed spectacles, dressed in gray suits, climbing the stairs with their backs straight, on their way to offices on the second floor. He saw the cleaners with their dungarees and pails full of soapy water and mops. He saw all of this in his imagination, none of it from the vibrations.

He climbed the stairs to Studio4Ward.

Chapter 7

He'd outdone himself this time - three beautiful women, all pissed at him at the same time, and one of them a fan until less than an hour ago. He stood in Cranbury's studio space, rummaging with his eyes - CIs weren't allowed to touch things while they were making referrals. Not that something as ephemeral as the rules had ever stopped Boston Jonson, but Cranbury's space was wide open, and three sets of eyes, all of them hostile and annoyed watched him from a place of hostility and annoyance. Still, he liked to think they were interested in what he was doing, fascinated by his unorthodox approach to investigative consulting. He put his hand above the back of Art Cranbury's folding beach chair. The metal showing through the plastic slats looked expensive, titanium, or something equally strong to hold the big man's weight.

He closed his eyes, relaxed his shoulders, and let his awareness drift slowly from his head, down through his chest, and into his tan dien. He breathed deeply, right down to his crotch, feeling the energy of the universe flowing through the top of his head and down to his toes as he breathed through his nose. He expelled the breath slowly through his mouth, visualizing the energy of the earth flowing up through his legs and abdomen and into his head. Within seconds, he was relaxed both physically and mentally. He was a vessel of calm, open to the music of Creation, the vibrations. Cranbury's thoughts were in his beach chair, the story of his life and the story of his death shivered in the vibrations around his chair. Cranbury's ghost called out for justice from the operating system of the universe. Boston opened his inner ear to the call and waited.

And waited.

After several minutes, he heard a loud female voice. "Do you have to hum so loud?" It was Fox. Boston snapped out of it. The three artists were staring at him, irritated, hostile. "We're trying to work here, you know. It's already hard enough to focus with Art dead and hanging on Andrea's wall."

Boston ignored her. He looked around Cranbury's space. The stains were undoubtedly dried barf. It lingered just under every few breaths of air. The ladies weren't exaggerating about the smell when Cranbury did a marathon sit-in. There was a large wooden trunk pushed up against the wall. The latch was down. It was unlocked. Strange, thought Boston, very trusting for a man who's biggest talent was making enemies. Beside the beach chair was a small table littered with tubes of paint, brushes, and a beer can. The easel was adjusted low so that Cranbury could paint while he was sitting. It faced out, showing off his latest work, his last work.

Up close, it didn't look as childish as from a distance. There were light tones and blends of color suggesting that the painter didn't just wipe paint on the canvas haphazardly, but might actually have tried to give a little depth to the painting. It was a beer can, slightly angled, hanging in white space, a bit wider than the real thing, the kind of beer can that Art Cranbury would love to have wrapped his

33

plump paws around. He'd even painted in all the small print info - 7.5 % alcohol, Dabst Breweries, Munchen Germany - but it was the label that interested Boston most. It showed a television set, the kind seen in old movies before the 2020s, before integrated wireless home com systems made standalone televisions, radios, and stereo systems as scarce as 8-tracks. It looked like it was tuned into a football game with little sticklike blue and white football players wearing helmets that were almost as big as their entire bodies. A football soared across the screen toward the white players' goal post. For some reason, Boston couldn't visualize Art Cranbury being a football fan, until he made out a small table facing the television. It had what looked like a beer can sitting on it.

He looked around the studio, aware of furtive glances from the three ladies who wanted the orange-haired freak out of their studio and the candy cane Art off their wall. There was no doubting it, Art Cranbury was a pig. It wasn't just the empty beer cans and pizza boxes strewn over the floor, it was the smell, the smell of rot and sweat and puke, the smell of someone with a hard-on to make everyone around him miserable. Whoever had nailed him to the wall had done the world a favor, maybe even the dead guy.

Each of the artists' studios afforded them two walls to display their work. Cranbury had been a prolific non-artist, filling his wall space with dozens of beer can paintings from different breweries with different labels. Boston looked closely at one of the labels - a beach with scythe-like waves and a sun with yellow rays. In the foreground sat a cooler with a beer can on its cover. The painting next to it showed a picnic basket with a beer can on its cover flap. Besides that, a canoe with full beer can holders. All the paintings were of things to do while drinking cans of beer.

Cranbury had a theme.

Chapter 8

"Cranbury had a theme," announced Boston. Fox stopped spreading a layer of light red, WhiteFeather stopped pulling staples out of the second moccasin, Crabbe stopped pouring water onto a canvas lying on the floor. They looked at him the way they would look at a fly stubbornly landing on the edge of their coffee mugs no matter how many times they swatted it away.

WhiteFeather clucked her tongue. "What the hell is that supposed to mean?"

Boston pointed at one of the paintings hanging askew on the wall. "He didn't just paint beer cans." He pointed at the one beside it. "He painted beer can themes, things you do when you're drinking cans of beer."

"Jonson," said WhiteFeather. "He painted beer cans! He wasn't an artist. He was a drunken slob who pretended to... "

"Even if he did have a theme," said Fox. "What does that have to do with anything?"

Boston thought for a moment. "I'm not sure. Just throwing it out there."

"You're not going to start humming again, are you?" Crabbe looked worried. "It's really irritating."

He ignored the remark. "How do you sign your paintings?"

"How do I what?"

"Sign your paintings? You sign them when you're finished, don't you?"

Shaking her head just enough to reveal her other eye, she pointed to a large blue canvas leaning against the wall behind her. In silver and gold Roman lettering across the bottom was the word CRABBE, almost a foot high. Boston noticed the same lettering on her other finished paintings. "I incorporate my name right into my paintings. It's *my* theme." Her hot soup voice was heavily spiced with sarcasm. Fox and WhiteFeather giggled.

He strolled over to Fox's studio. Dozens of large and small paintings, mostly portraits, hung in neat rows and columns, all of them signed with just one letter: M.

"You sign everything with an M?"

Fox glared at him. She was short, but perfectly proportioned and beautiful in a stand-offish way that Boston suspected was shyness. Her stand-offishness had nothing to do with shyness at the moment though. She was cheesed off. Glaring. Her voice grated with aggravation. "Yes, Mr. Jonson. Everything. And it's not even my theme."

"What exactly is your theme?"

"People I meet in my dreams."

Boston smiled. "Maybe you'll dream about me someday."

"I don't do nightmares." She smiled defiantly.

"So... " He let it hang out there for a moment, until the defiance drained out of her smile, and the smile drained off her face. She cocked her head downward and to the side in a beautifully rendered *So? So what?* gesture.

"So, you think it's amusing to paint Christ as a barber shop pole?"

If there's one thing Boston Jonson was good at, it was making people look at him as though he'd just popped out of Dimension X with three heads and a furry tail. That's exactly how the three Studio4Ward artists were staring at him now. He could almost feel the extra head on each shoulder.

WhiteFeather looked like she was about to spring from her stool and attack him with the pliers. "What are you saying, Jonson? That Art is Christ? That... ?"

"Downstairs." He stared deep into Fox's eyes, savoring the confusion he saw thrashing behind her big brown irises.

"Downstairs, what?" she finally mustered.

"You drew candy stripes on Christ in the Rio De Janeiro poster at Backstreet. You signed it with an M, the same M as on your paintings."

Fox squinted her eyes, flashing equal amounts of annoyance and confusion. She shook her head. "So what? I painted stripes on a poster. Eric knows I did it. That's why he moved it behind the counter, so that people could see it. He thought it was cool. What's the big deal?"

And he led me to believe that he didn't know who'd done it.

Boston pointed his thumb at the corpse on the wall. "You did the same to Art... " In a single movement, he curled his thumb in and pointed his finger at Fox. "... after you killed him."

She didn't even blink. "Oh, it's back to me again, is it?"

"My turn next!" called WhiteFeather.

"Then me again! After all, he's hanging in my space."

"Then, of course, you would have needed accomplices to get the body onto the wall." He swung his gaze slowly over the other two, smiling sardonically for the fifth time in one day. He looked back at Fox. "But you didn't kill him."

"Gee, thanks." She turned her head back to her painting, mumbling something about some people making up their minds.

Boston walked over to the corpse. He could understand why the ladies would want it gone. It was gross. But he wondered about the living Art Cranbury, about the empty pit at the center of the man's life, a pit so deep that not all the beer and pizza in the world could fill it. And he wondered about the man's true art, the art of making people hate him. It took a tremendous amount of self-hatred to perfect that art as well as he had. And now he was dead. The world no longer had Art Cranbury to inflict pain on others and on himself. Oh well, to hell with him. He was out of his misery, and the world was a better place without him, no matter how he'd gotten that way.

What interested Boston at the moment was the stuff covering his body. He leaned forward and smelled.

Just as he'd thought.

Oil paint.

"Ms Crabbe? Do you paint with oils?"

Impatiently, Crabbe looked up at him. She was swirling water in the center of a canvas. The water rolled over swatches of red, green and yellow inside a border of blue and white paint. "Do you think I'd be doing *this* with oil paint? I use acrylics."

"And does WhiteFeather use paint?"

"No. Not much. Rarely. And yes, that's oil paint on Art. A lot of oil paint. It's his paint. He keeps... kept it in the trunk in his studio. He used to open it and brag about how he could afford to use all the oil paint he wanted. It used to drive Marie... " She swished water over the paint, washing it across the surface of the canvas. She let out an angry sigh. "Marie uses oil. It costs a fortune. She can just barely afford to buy enough for her work." She pointed the canvas toward Art. "There's about five hundred dollars' worth on that body." She put the canvas on the floor and stood up. "Jonson?"

"Yes?"

Her voice was barely a whisper. "Marie killed a spider once in her studio. She looked at the smashed-up body and then ran for the washroom to throw up. That's how she feels about killing things. She couldn't have killed Art."

Boston gave a non-committal nod. "Of course, the spider didn't try to humiliate her for not being able to afford oil paint."

"Asshole." She said it so matter-of-fact and neutral, like stating a fact.

Sometimes, we're what works.

He walked back to Art's studio. The lid to the trunk was closed. He looked around. None of the ladies were watching. He raised a sandaled foot to the trunk and lifted the lid with his right toe. The trunk was filled with tubes of paint and unused brushes. Scattered over the top were empty tubes of red and white paint. He could see by the swipe marks that they'd been wiped clean of fingerprints.

"Isn't there something about you not being allowed to touch anything?" called WhiteFeather from across the room. Boston blushed and let the lid fall quickly back down.

"Yeah, like, isn't that tampering with the evidence?" Fox made a face at him and stuck her tongue out. Crabbe smirked quietly as she dripped water from a rag onto the canvas.

He decided to pick on the fiber artist. He strolled casually over to her studio, ducking under the snakeskin chandelier. WhiteFeather looked up at him, squinting her eyes ruefully. He ignored the rue, and looked around her studio, amazed by all the... stuff. There was stuff everywhere - workbenches piled high with cellophane bags, glittering gift bags, and brightly colored shopping bags, all full of stuff, every imaginable kind of stuff: wooden corks, feathers, beads, swatches of material. There were big bottles filled bones and hair, boxes stuffed with old jewelry, spangles, and lace. There were pots, a sewing machine, vice grips, bottles with chemicals. In the corner, several boxes overflowed with thick and thin coils of rope. A headless leather manikin draped in what looked like a gown from the 1800s stood behind a chair crammed with still more bottles and bags.

The wall over her workbench was hung with dozens of large dolls, and not the kind of doll you would give to your young daughter. Heavy black stitching showed where the thick hide-like fabric of their bodies had been sewn together, giving them that fresh just-brought-back-from-death look. Some had arms made from large feathers, giving them

41

bird-like countenances, though their heads were the skulls of small animals like rabbits or raccoons. They were at once disturbing and mesmerizing.

"Kill them yourself?"

"What?" She held the pliers with a menacing dagger-like grip.

"How do you get all the bones?"

"People bring them to me," she spat. "People who believe in what I'm doing."

Boston nodded. "Bet you'd like to use Art's head in one of your dolls."

WhiteFeather's nostrils flared. Her eyes almost bulged. Her face flushed deep red. She stood up and pointed the pliers at Boston. "I'd like to put your head in that vice grip... " She pointed the pliers at the vice grip attached to her workbench and then back at Boston. "... and squeeze the shit you have for brains out through your ears!"

Boston remained cool. "Did you know that pointing pliers at a CI while in the process of referring is punishable by up to ten hours of community work?"

WhiteFeather cocked her head to the side, looked almost astounded. "And what's the punishment for CIs who outstay their welcome and tamper with evidence before they make a referral." Her lips curled into a snarkey smile.

He let it bounce off.

He looked around and noticed a painting in a corner just below a doll with thick black human hair spouting out of the skull of what looked like some type of rodent. There was something about the painting. He walked slowly past the angry artist, who had stopped pointing the pliers at him - the dissuasive power of community work - and looked closer. It was abstract, a rectangular pattern of bright blues and yellows bordering a pink space containing abstract shapes that seemed vaguely familiar. The painting reminded Boston of something, but he couldn't put his finger on it.

"What's this?"

WhiteFeather sat back on her stool to pull more staples. "It's a painting." Her voice smacked of resignation. He was starting to break these people.

"Who did it?"

"It's one of Andrea's studies. She does small scale studies like that before beginning a major series."

Boston turned his head in the direction of Crabbe's studio. Large white canvasses stretched over wooden frames leaned against most of the wall opposite him. Small paintings and clippings from magazines and newspapers were barely visible in the spaces between the canvasses. On his way over to her studio, the snakeskin chandelier brushed against the side of his head. It chilled him.

He went straight to the small things peeking out from between the blank canvasses. The paintings were in various states of completion, some looked like finished works; others were mostly colorful outlines. They were like monitors with abstract graphics on their screens, except the navigation and tool bars bordering the interface looked more like lettering than buttons. There were nine of them, all of them similar to the one in WhiteFeather's studio. There was something oddly familiar about them.

"These are interesting, Ms Crabbe."

The artist looked up at him.

"Is this a new direction for you?"

"What makes you say that?" She sounded either curious or guarded - he wasn't sure which.

"It doesn't look like there's going to be room for a foot high signature on any of these."

She smiled, almost relieved. "Maybe I've decided to change my theme."

"Did Cranbury ever make sexual advances on you?"

She might have just eaten a worm or a live frog from the look that crossed her face. She spoke slowly and venomously. "He sat in his chair pretending to paint and leered at us constantly, but he never tried anything." She took a deep breath. "We would have thrown him out the window. I think he knew that."

"And you never led him on?"

Fury exploded in her eyes. She almost screamed. "What? Lead him on! Look at him!" She pointed at the corpse. "Do you think I would lead something like... that on? Art was the most repulsive human being on the face of his planet! I'd rather chew my right arm off!"

Boston ignored her. He walked up close to the dead man, looking closely up and down his sides. The paint seemed to be thicker on his hips and the sides of his face. Crabbe glared at him, fuming, as he walked past and took a palette knife from the workbench behind her. He walked back to the corpse and scraped a long swath of paint from the top of the waist to the top of the leg. The area around the hip was badly bruised, almost black. He scraped paint from one side of Cranbury's head. Black and blue.

"More tampering with the evidence?" WhiteFeather craned her neck toward Boston, school marmish. "Stepping out of your sphere of authority, aren't you?" He ignored her.

Time to heat things up.

"How important is your new theme?"

She cocked her head forward, questioningly. "My new theme?"

"Six packs."

"What are you talking about?"

"You have a painting in WhiteFeather's studio."

"So?"

"It's a small one, a study before you start a series. A small one like those." He pointed at the paintings peeking out from between the stacks of canvasses. "Have you begun your series?"

She looked suspicious, cautious. "I... I'm not sure if I'm going to work on that series."

"Why?"

"It... I don't know." She fussed with her hair, pulled it back, exposing both eyes. Fear and confusion lurked in those peepers. "Sometimes an idea seems good, but then you work on it... that's what the small paintings are for... to see if the idea really will work. This one didn't."

"Why?"

"I don't know! It just didn't!"

"Did you tell Art Cranbury about your idea?"

Silence. Stunned silence. A gasp in time. The three ladies stared at him, seemingly without

45

breathing. He tilted his head to the right, raising an eyebrow. "Did you?"

"When he first moved in. Before we knew what he was like."

"And?"

"I told him about an idea I was working on, something new." Her fear and confusion seemed to have melted away. She seemed almost excited. "I was going to call it Canned Beer Culture, a series of paintings showing the relationship between canned beer and popular culture. It was going to be a complete departure from the work I've been doing up till now." Her shoulders slumped. The excitement drained out of her face.

"He stole your idea, didn't he?"

She sighed deeply. "I trusted the bastard. He started doing those... things." She pointed towards Cranbury's studio, at the painting on the easel. "The idea was to use labels from beer cans as windows into culture. I told him about the different types of activities I wanted to use, an historical collage, going back to the days of television."

"Andrea!" called WhiteFeather. "Maybe you shouldn't be telling him this."

Without taking his eyes of Crabbe, he said, "Interrupting a CI in the course of questioning a witness while making a referral is a serious offense punishable by up five hours of community work."

WhiteFeather rolled her eyes.

"He stole your idea."

Tears rolled over the young woman's face as she nodded yes.

"But he was a nobody in the arts. Why didn't you just do your paintings? Nobody but the people here would have seen his."

She sniffled loudly and took a deep breath to calm herself. "He's rich. Slob and greasy little asshole that he was, he was rich. He told me that he was going to buy an art gallery and put his paintings on display. He dared me to finish my series and put them in a gallery. He said he would spend thousands on an advertising campaign for his opening, bribe a couple of reviewers, make some hefty donations to the right people in the arts community. He said that it wouldn't matter how crappy his paintings were. If the public were told they were great, then they would be great. And he said that, if I did my paintings, he would publicly accuse me of stealing his idea, maybe even sue me."

"So you killed him."

Terror raced through her eyes. "No! It wasn't like that!"

"You hipped him to death."

Her eyes were wide, mouth quivering, sweat beading across her forehead. "He asked for it."

"Asked for it?"

She sat down on a stool, careful not to put her foot on the canvas she'd been watering. After a few deep breaths, her shoulders slooped and calmed. "Some of us were out drinking beer last night. I must have had about ten or more. On my way home, I remembered that I'd left my apartment keys on my workbench, so I came here to get them. Art was here. He was drunk, as usual. He said something about us being friends and I told him to go to hell."

47

She wrapped her arms around herself and shivered. She breathed deeply a few more times. Her hands were shaking. "He said that was no way to talk to someone who was just going to do something good for me. I asked what he was talking about and he said that he'd been thinking about what he said about stealing my idea. He said there was something I could do for him that could change his mind. I screamed that I wasn't having sex with him no matter how many ideas he stole from me."

"Andrea!" WhiteFeather was on her feet, rushing over to Crabbe's studio. She leaned down and hugged her. Both artists started crying. From her studio, Fox's eyes bored malevolently into Boston. "You don't have to talk about any of this," said WhiteFeather. She glanced at Boston. "Especially to him."

'Him' waited patiently. After a few minutes, Crabbe calmed again. WhiteFeather pulled a stool over and sat beside her. "He said he didn't want to have sex with me, that he'd been watching me do my hip thing with the other girls and with some of the men who came in here. He said he wanted to be hipped."

"That would explain the bruises on his hip," said Boston.

"I thought he was crazy at first, but he told me that nobody had ever done something like that to him, that'd he'd always been treated like a piece of toast. He said 'toast.' I mean, I was drunk. I started to feel sorry for him. Then, he told me that if I hipped him a few times, that he wouldn't steal my idea, that he would destroy the paintings he'd done, and that he would even help me get my paintings into a major gallery in New York or Paris." She slapped both hands onto her knees. "And then he came out with the clincher. He said that he would move out of Studio4Ward."

WhiteFeather's jaw did the proverbial 'drop in shock.' Fox's arm fell to her side, painting a red swath across her knee-high sun dress.

"I asked him if he was serious. He said that he was getting bored hanging around the studio anyway, that he was thinking about moving to the Bahamas or to South America. I was that drunk that I believed him. I said let's go for it. He struggled up out his chair and came over to my studio. I hipped him lightly. He said I'd have to do better than that, so I hipped him harder. He asked me if I really wanted him out of the studio and I screamed yes. I was drunk. I was so drunk. I hipped him with everything I had and then again. And then I realized... I mean, I don't know how he did it so fast that I didn't even see it coming. He was naked. I was trying not to look at him when I hipped him, but still... " She looked at Boston imploringly. "He was naked. And then he was on his knees, begging me to hip him in the head. He said he wasn't moving anywhere until I hipped him... in the head." She shook like jello. WhiteFeather put a hand on her shoulder and was just about to say something when Crabbe continued. "All the anger I felt about him stealing my idea, all the rage from all the nights and days that he sat in his chair belching and farting and leering and playing that awful music so loud that none of us could think... it all exploded. It exploded." A blank, lost expression crept into her eyes. "With everything I had, I hipped that fat bastard in the side of the head." She went quiet, staring at the wall, eyes emotionless, drained. "He just... fell over. I called his name a few times, but he didn't answer. I went over to him and nudged him. He didn't move. I saw his face and I almost threw up. It was then that I knew he was dead." She began crying quietly. WhiteFeather stood and put her arms around her, patting her back, telling her everything would be OK, that it wasn't her fault, that she was just doing what Art told her to do. That it was an accident.

"It was manslaughter," said Boston.

Again, he was the focal point for venomous stares. But he was used to it. He reveled in it. "Accidents are generally reported as soon as they happen. You nailed the guy to the wall. You killed him and then you nailed him."

Crabbe stared at him, expressionless.

"That was my idea," said a male voice from the door. It was Hill. "I was downstairs filling Internet orders when I heard a loud thump on the floor. It was late, so I came upstairs to check it out. I saw Art naked on the floor and Andrea leaning over him, crying. She told me what happened. She wanted to call the police, but we were both afraid she would be charged with murder, spend the rest of her life doing community work. Then we saw the bright side."

"The bright side?" Boston thumbed the body behind him. "This is the bright side?"

"Studio4Ward has been going through a slump since Art moved in. Nobody's been getting any serious work done. I've been losing business steadily because of Art's lousy music driving my customers away. Even the other studios downstairs have been losing business. Art's been a curse on this building. So I figured, why not let Art be a blessing."

"You nailed him up for the publicity." Boston gave the shop owner a look of disgust. "He was a human being." He looked back at the candy striped dead man and frowned. "At some point or another."

"It would have been the only useful thing he'd ever done," said Hill.

Boston nodded agreement grudgingly. "How did you get him up there."

Hill pointed up at the fan in the ceiling. "We borrowed some of WhiteFeather's rope and made a sling and tied the rope to the axel in the fan." WhiteFeather arched her brows at the mention of her rope. "Those fans are over a hundred and fifty years old and were built to last forever. We used it as a pulley to help lift the body up and then swung him over close enough for me to nail his head to the wall with one of WhiteFeather's spikes."

WhiteFeather was beginning to look a little pissed by now. She looked back and forth between Hill and Crabbe. Crabbe looked at her pleadingly. "If they tried to pin it on you because of the rope and the spikes, I was going to step up and tell them it was me. Honestly, WhiteFeather, we weren't trying to frame you or anything."

WhiteFeather thought about this for a moment, nodded and smiled. Both women hugged. Hill shrugged. "It seemed like a good idea at the time."

Boston shot him a condescending look. "And what did you think would be the referral on a corpse nailed to the wall?"

Hill shrugged again, looking like a big guilty kid. "I don't know. Suicide?"

Boston's wallet started buzzing. He ignored it. "Ms Fox!"

Fox seemed almost to wilt. She clamped her teeth together, looking like she'd just been caught with both hands in the cookie jar.

"That seemed like the thing to do... as well," she said. "I was coming home from the party, passed the studio, saw the lights were off, which meant that Art wasn't here, so I came upstairs. I don't know why... just to stand in here without that piece of shit leering at me for a change. I saw Art hanging on Andrea's wall as soon as I came in." Her eyes began to moisten. "He used to make fun of me for being so skimpy with my paint. Once, he emptied two large tubes of it into a pizza box and swished the paint around with his hands and said that he was doing a fifty dollar finger painting and wouldn't I just love to afford that? He used enough paint to last me months." Her eyes grew hard, angry. "I thought about that when I saw him up there. I went to his trunk and took out all the red and white paint and two of his expensive brushes and painted him." She sniffed. "He always said he was art."

"And you just happened paint the bruised areas thicker?"

She bit her lower lip lightly. "I saw a bruise like his on someone after Andrea hipped him at one of our parties. I didn't know if she had anything to do with his death, but I thought that, if she did, then maybe I could cover for her. I was really drunk at the time."

Crabbe and Fox exchanged sympathetic glances. Hill sat down on the floor, elbows propped on his knees, hands clapped to both sides of his head. "Are we going to spend the rest of our lives doing community work?" There was genuine regret in his voice, fear. Community work.

Boston's wallet buzzed. He took it from his pocket and opened it. Laurel was furious. "I need that referral... "

"It's ready," said Boston.

"It's ready? Now?"

"Yep."

"What, then?"

"Suicide."

THE END

Don't miss Boston Jonson in his first full-length novel - Murder by Burger

Acknowledgements

Thanks to the folks at Studio4Ward and Backstreet Records for taking their characterizations in this story in good humor and not nailing me to a wall and painting me candy stripe blues:

WhiteFeather, Studio4Ward
(http://www.vrvgallery.com/whitefeather)

Eric Hill, Backstreet Records
(http://www.backstreetrecords.blogspot.com)

Andrea Crabbe, formerly in residence at Mazerolle Gallery, a few doors down from Backstreet (www.andreacrabbe.com)

Marie Fox, Studio4Ward

Mazerolle Gallery
(http://www.freewebs.com/mazerollegallery)

Cover photo by Andrea Crabbe - taken at Studio4Ward

Visit Biff at www.biffmitchell.com